P9-CNF-643

THE FRIGHTFUL STORY OF
HARRY WALFISH

A Richard Jackson Book
Liber jackson richard

THE FRIGHTFUL STORY OF HARRY WALFISH

STORY AND PICTURES BY BRIAN FLOCA

ORCHARD BOOKS • NEW YORK

Floca, Brian
FIC   The frightful story
FLO   Harry Walfish

Copyright © 1997 by Brian Floca
All rights reserved. No part of this book may be reproduced or transmitted in any form or by any
means, electronic or mechanical, including photocopying, recording, or by any information
storage or retrieval system, without permission in writing from the Publisher.

Orchard Books, 95 Madison Avenue, New York, NY 10016

Manufactured in the United States of America. Printed by Barton Press, Inc.
Bound by Horowitz/Rae. Book design by Mina Greenstein.

The text of this book is set in 14 point Bitstream ITC Quorum Medium. The illustrations are ink
line and watercolor reproduced in full color.

10 9 8 7 6 5 4 3 2 1

Library of Congress Cataloging-in-Publication Data
Floca, Brian. The frightful story of Harry Walfish / story and pictures by Brian Floca.   p.   cm.
Summary: When her class goes ape on a school visit to the Natural History Museum, a wily teacher
tells the tale of a rambunctious former classmate of her own who found himself left behind in
the museum after dark.
ISBN 0-531-30008-0.   ISBN 0-531-33008-7 (lib. bdg.)
[1. Museums—Fiction. 2. Behavior—Fiction.]   I. Title.   PZ7.F6579Fr   1997   [E]—dc20   96-42153

FOR

Fellow former
tenants of
230 Ives.

Ubi amici, ibi opes.

M<small>S.</small> L<small>EONARD-</small>B<small>RAKTHURST</small> cleared her throat again. "Now, class, let me tell you the story of Harry Walfish."

She had tried to tell us the nesting habits of the Himalayan white-crested laughing thrush, but I guess we were making too much noise for that. The whole class was shoehorned into one small room at the Natural History Museum, and maybe all those old stuffed animals inspired some imitations.

Monkeys did seem to be on the minds of a few kids.

And Krissy Kearns was mimicking the Indian elephant, although I thought she sounded more like a horse.

Jimmy Frickle pretended to be a mako shark, which wasn't so loud in itself but did get a scream out of Glenn Frankel.

Alberto Hernandez impersonated a bluefin tuna. No one knew a fish could be so noisy, but Alberto seemed convinced.

Over by the platypus exhibit, Deirdre Sullivan developed her theories on how one of those might sound if it was really agitated. Jenny Herdstop thought she was choking.

I suppose the racket added up. But Ms. Leonard-Brakthurst pressed on.

More loudly she said, "Harry Walfish could create a ruckus and a din and a tumult that would make you all seem as quiet as these stuffed animals. He terrorized my class, when I was your age, and turned our teacher, Mrs. Grimmer, into a great supporter of early retirement for educators."

We quieted just a bit. Might Harry Walfish prove more interesting than the Himalayan white-crested laughing thrush?

"Poor old Nelda Grimmer," said Ms. Leonard-Brakthurst. "When she brought our class to museums like this one—once, to this very museum—Harry treated them like playgrounds. The minute we walked through the door, he sprinted away to accomplish some mischief.

"He pried open exhibit cases and rearranged the labels on the animals, so that the water buffalo's label read PENGUIN and the penguin's label read SQUID and so forth. Then he yanked the fragile animals out of their cases and ran with them as if they were footballs or kites or hockey sticks, all the while singing unrepeatably vile little songs so loudly some swore he'd been born with a third lung, although that was never proven.

"Mrs. Grimmer endured these and worse antics as best she could. She was forever tracking Harry down, catching him in the middle of one disaster or another, and trying to rein him back into the class. But Harry always slipped away again. And finally Mrs. Grimmer cracked.

"When the time came for the museum to close, Harry Walfish was still off on his own, who knows where, and Mrs. Grimmer, weary, exhausted Nelda Grimmer, did not search him out. After it was all over, she told the police she hadn't thought of him because she hadn't noticed he was missing. But one always noticed if Harry Walfish was missing. Things seemed so *quiet*. In any case, at the end of the day, the rest of the class filed out of the museum, and Harry Walfish was left behind."

"Was he alone?" asked Susie Grumm.

"All alone," said Ms. Leonard-Brakthurst.

"Was it dark?" asked Andy Morris.

"Very," said Ms. Leonard-Brakthurst.

"Was he scared?" asked Roni Pitkin.

Ms. Leonard-Brakthurst eyed us carefully, smiled gently, and continued. "Listen," she said.

"All we know about that night is what Harry told us, once he could talk about it. He said that after he'd run through the museum, whooping and hollering to the point of exhaustion, he realized the doors were bolted and the lights were put out and he was alone in the dim blue evening. Alone except for the animals in their glass cases, staring out with their glass eyes.

"It could have been an adventure, an opportunity to pry into crevices he failed to reach while the museum was open. But out of the corners of his eyes, did he see movements? Did that ear twitch? Did that tail swish? Did that tongue flick?

"You might become a bit nervous in such a situation. Harry Walfish did.

BENGAL TIGER
Felis tigris linnaeus

"So he found a chair near the entrance. He decided to wait, quietly, until Mrs. Grimmer or his parents missed him and realized where he was. He sat there bored and uneasy, until, to his surprise, he heard the fluttering of small wings. There seemed to be a bird loose in the museum, a rufous-rumped woodhewer. *Xiphorhynchus erythropygius*, I believe.''

Jake Webster asked, ''How did it get in the building?''

''That's what Harry wondered,'' said Ms. Leonard-Brakthurst. ''Then it occurred to him that the bird had not entered the building, but had *escaped* from an exhibit case.

"And suddenly the room blossomed with birds of all colors and sizes, squawking and singing and stirring the air with their wings. You can imagine, class, how this must have startled Harry.

"Then the room emptied as quickly as it had filled. The birds flew like arrows out every door save one, and through that one door Harry heard something like the purr of a small helpless kitten, but with the volume turned up, *up, UP!*

"Slowly, his eyes never leaving that door, Harry backed away from that noise, deeper and deeper into the museum. Backward he went through the next room. Backward he walked through a third room, until— *Thud*. Something blocked his path. Something large.

"Carefully, gently, he turned. He found himself staring at the giant Alaskan moose." Ms. Leonard-Brakthurst cleared her throat. *"And the moose stared back."*

Carefully, gently, the whole class turned. Did we see, around a corner, down a hallway, through a door, a large and mooselike shape?

Ms. Leonard-Brakthurst said, "The Alaskan moose, by which I mean the *Alces gigas*, the largest member of the Cervidae, or the deer family, dipped his heavy head and looked at Harry with eyes as large as eight balls. He shook his mighty antlers, antlers that grow five to six feet across in mature males, and he bellowed, a bellow louder than the horn sections of many metropolitan orchestras.

"And Harry, having been stared into and bellowed at by an old, dead, stuffed moose, ran out of that room. He ran past things that should have been sitting quietly in cases but that now scurried and sniffed and pawed about—tree frogs, a warthog, an ostrich, and a Bactrian camel, to name just a few.

"A long-tongued fruit bat, or *Macroglossus lagochilus*, dived at Harry from the ceiling, but Harry sprinted on, to the edge of collapse. Finally he had run as far as his legs would take him."

"And where was he then?" asked Samantha Rai.

"Where are we now?" asked Ms. Leonard-Brakthurst.

"The monkey room?" said Samantha Rai.

"The monkey room! Imagine," said Ms. Leonard-Brakthurst, bowing her legs and raising her arms above her head, "all these monkeys, from the largest orangutan, or *Pongo pygmaeus*, to the smallest pygmy marmoset, or *Callithrix pygmaea*, each with beady eyes and yellow teeth and groping hands, hopping about—*screech, screech, screech!* Imagine the ape, his fists pounding his great barrel chest—*thud, thud, thud!* Imagine poor Harry Walfish, surrounded by dancing beasts, alone, all alone in the dark night!"

We imagined.

"Around midnight Mrs. Grimmer and the Walfishes finally arrived with the curator and a police officer, *Homo sapiens* each one of them. With flashlights they searched the museum until they found Harry just over here, inside the exhibit case where the howler monkey, or *Alouatta seniculus*, belongs. He had apparently shut himself inside, and the case had somehow been encircled by animals that, when the Walfishes arrived, seemed very still, and quiet, and lifeless.

"Harry was rushed home, fed hot soup, put to bed, and he seemed all right, more or less. Few believed his story, once he finally told it, but no one could really explain how those stuffed monkeys ended up with their faces pressed against the case to which Harry had fled. A friend saw him recently and said that he's grown into a quiet man with a quiet job. On the bright side he's recently worked up the nerve to purchase a pet hamster. A *Mesocricetus auratus*."

Ms. Leonard-Brakthurst gathered her breath.

"Well," she said finally, "I'm not saying I absolutely believe every single word of that. I do, though, find it worth bearing in mind as our visit continues. Don't you all?"

We looked at the howler monkey. We looked at Ms. Leonard-Brakthurst. We nodded.

Ms. Leonard-Brakthurst eyed us carefully and smiled. "Now, class," she went on, "is there anybody here who is curious about the nesting habits of the Himalayan white-crested laughing thrush?"